Deleted

HOPEWELL SCHOOL
LIBRARY

W9-BME-348

HOPEWELL SCHOOL
LIBRARY

HOPEWELL SCHOOL
LIBRARY

HOPEWELL SCHOOL
LIBRARY

HOPEWELL SCHOOL
LIBRARY

HOPEWELL SCHOOL
LIBRARY

Kathi Appelt

WATERMELON DAY

Illustrated by Dale Gottlieb

Henry Holt and Company · New York

E
APP
1-29-02
225/0652

Henry Holt and Company, LLC, *Publishers since 1866*
115 West 18th Street, New York, New York 10011

Henry Holt is a registered trademark of Henry Holt and Company, LLC
Text copyright © 1996 by Kathi Appelt. Illustrations copyright © 1996 by Dale Gottlieb.
All rights reserved. Published in Canada by Fitzhenry & Whiteside Ltd.,
195 Allstate Parkway, Markham, Ontario L3R 4T8.

Library of Congress Cataloging-in-Publication Data
Appelt, Kathi.
Watermelon Day / Kathi Appelt; illustrated by Dale Gottlieb.
Summary: Young Jesse waits all summer for her watermelon to ripen.
[1. Watermelons—Fiction.] I. Gottlieb, Dale, ill. II. Title.
PZ7.A6455Wat 1994 [E]—dc20 95-38199

ISBN 0-8050-2304-6
First Edition—1996
Printed in the United States of America on acid-free paper. ∞
3 5 7 9 10 8 6 4 2
The artist used oil pastel on rag paper to create the illustrations for this book.

To Ken, who has his own
sweet song   —K.A.

For Nanny and Harry
          —D. G.

*T*hat watermelon grew in the corner of the patch where the fence posts met. Jesse found it early one day while pulling weeds. It was not as big as her fist, but it was bigger than the other melons still hiding beneath their mamas' fuzzy leaves.

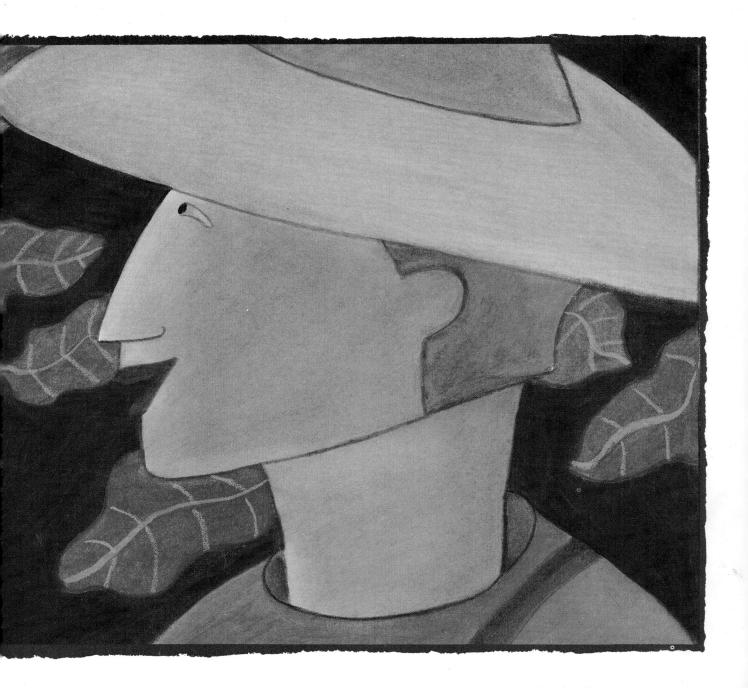

When she showed it to Pappy, he smiled. "Yep, it'll be a big one all right. It'll be just right for a Watermelon Day."

"A Watermelon Day!"

Jesse knew what that meant. There would be
cousins, big and small. Mama's peach ice cream.
Innings and innings of softball. Relay races and
apple-bobbing. Uncle Ike with his banjo.

Finally, to top it all, ice-cold watermelon—the
biggest one from the patch.

Thinking about it made Jesse's mouth water.

"How long till it's ready, Pappy?" she asked.

"Got a whole summer to go yet," he answered.

Jesse looked at the small melon. It was round
and snug in the sand. She smiled.

Every day Jesse walked up and down the rows of the patch. When she got to her melon, she knelt beside it and put her ear against its dark green rind. She patted it with her palm. At first it made a thick, dull sound, like Pappy's boots when

he dropped them on the front porch. But as the days passed, the sound grew brighter.

Jesse patted the other melons, too. Some sounded dull. Some sounded bright. But hers had the sweetest song.

"How much longer, Pappy?" she asked.
"Not much longer now," he answered.

The summer days grew longer. Jesse's watermelon got riper. Its stripes began to zig and zag.

Jesse waited. She waited until the days were so hot she had to wear shoes so her feet wouldn't blister in the sand. So hot the air wrinkled up like an unironed shirt. So hot that hardly anything moved except the flies.

She waited until she thought she and her watermelon might both burst from the sheer waiting of it all.

One morning, when the relatives were coming, Jesse asked, "How much longer, Pappy?" Pappy looked at Jesse. He looked at the watermelon patch. He looked at the blue summer sky. "Well," he answered, "this looks like a Watermelon Day."

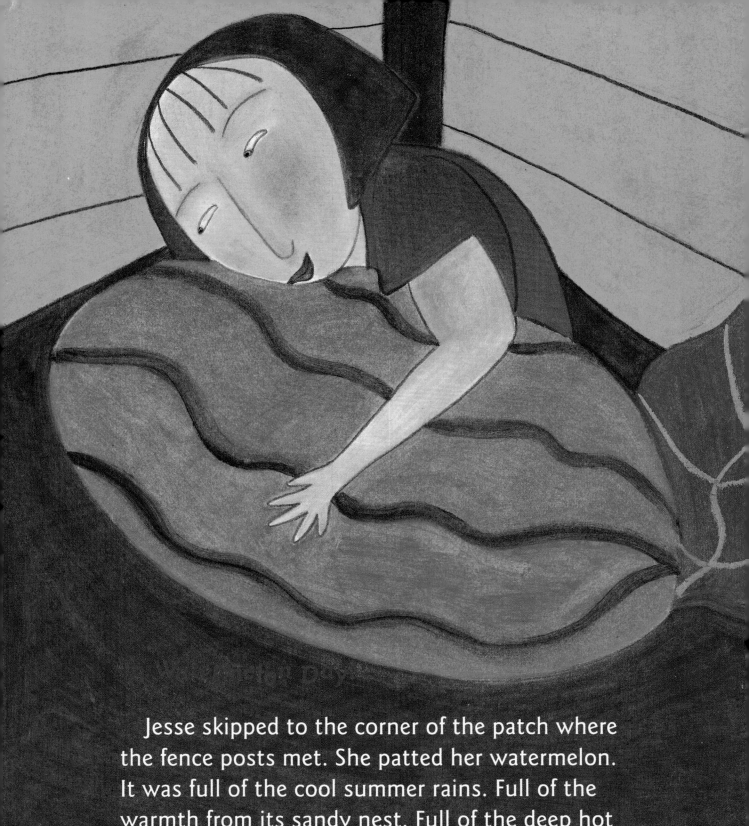

Jesse skipped to the corner of the patch where the fence posts met. She patted her watermelon. It was full of the cool summer rains. Full of the warmth from its sandy nest. Full of the deep hot sun.

Pappy cut the ropelike vine with his pocketknife
and carried the melon out of the patch, past the
front porch and down to the lake. He set it in the
cold, cold water. There it floated, right along the
edge, beneath the deep blue shade of the
weeping willow tree.

"How long will it take, Pappy?" asked Jesse.
"Most of the day," he answered. "There's a
whole summer's worth of heat inside it."

Jesse's watermelon floated all that hot day long.
Willow branches dipped up and down, testing the
icy water. That melon floated while the cousins came.

It floated while Mama dished out peach ice cream.
It floated through a game of softball and several
relay races. It even floated while Uncle Ike
played "Turkey in the Straw."

And all the while Jesse thought about it, her mouth watered.

Watermelon, watermelon.

"How much longer, Pappy?" she asked.
"Oh, it's not ready yet," he answered.

The day stretched and stretched like a lazy ol'
cat. Jesse waited and waited.

She waited through more innings of softball.
She waited through apple-bobbing. She waited
through freeze-tag. She waited through Uncle
Ike's rendition of "Stars and Stripes Forever."

At last the sun began to sink. The sweat dried on
Jesse's neck. The lake shimmered. "How much longer,
Pappy?" she asked. Pappy looked at Jesse. He looked
at the sinking sun. He looked at the shimmery lake.
"I think it's good and cold now," he answered.

Jesse hopped. She skipped. She danced all the way to the lake. Pappy lifted the melon out of the icy water and carried it to the front porch, where he set it down.

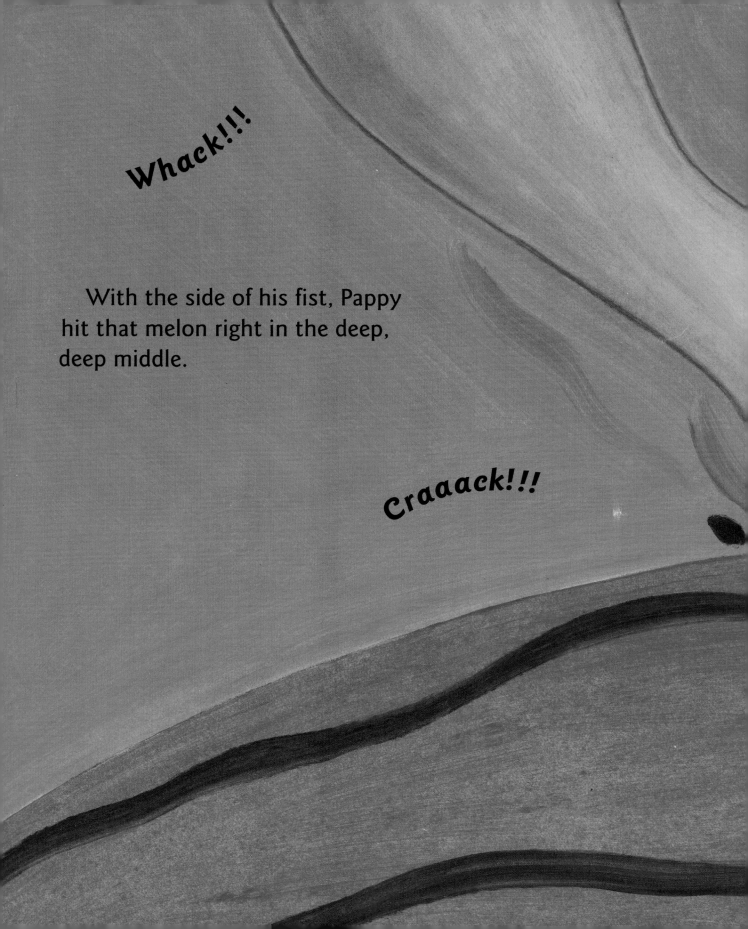

Whack!!!

With the side of his fist, Pappy hit that melon right in the deep, deep middle.

Craaack!!!

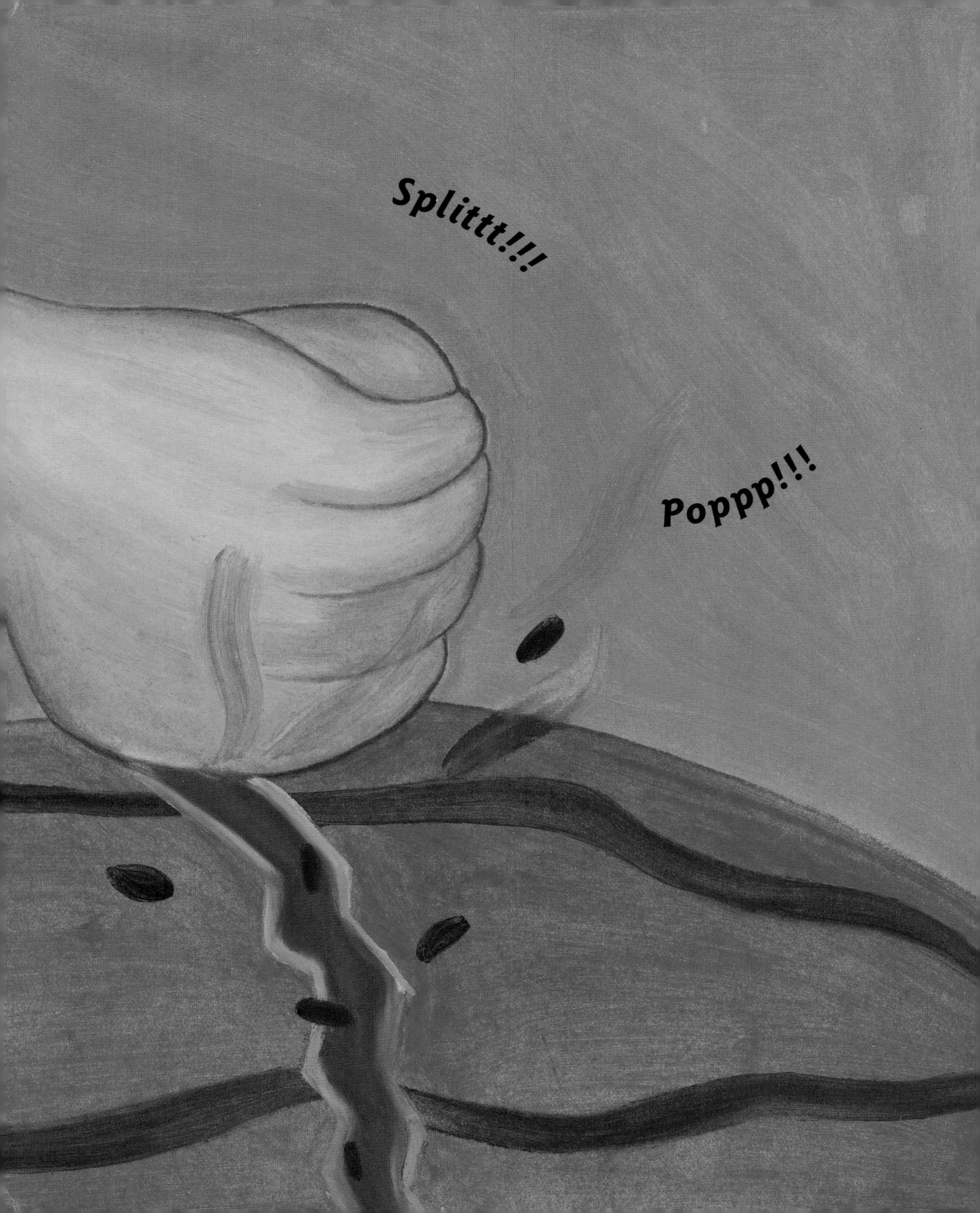
Splittt!!!
Poppp!!!

Red, red juice ran down Jesse's chin. It ran down
her hand and between her fingers. It splashed
onto her toes.

That melon was sweet. Sweet as the summer rain.
Sweet as a nighttime song. That melon was cold. Cold
as a puppy's nose. Cold as the deep blue lake.

Jesse smiled. She danced. She spit watermelon
seeds into the sky. She sang a watermelon song.

Watermelon, watermelon.

It's a Watermelon Day!

HOPEWELL SCHOOL
LIBRARY

HOPEWELL SCHOOL
LIBRARY

E
APP

HOPEWELL SCHOOL LIBRARY

Watermelon Day.

22510652

E
APP

Appelt, Kathi.

Watermelon Day.

DATE			

HOPEWELL SCHOOL LIBRARY
TAUNTON, MA 02780

BAKER & TAYLOR